# Dragonsong
## A Fable for the New Millennium

Written by Russell Young
Illustrated by Civi Cheng

SHEN'S
BOOKS

www.shens.com    Fremont, California

here was once a young dragon in China named Chiang-An. He was young and small for a dragon, being only 224 years old when many others were several thousand years old. While the other dragons flew from place to place in China, Chiang-An loved one little village in the southeast corner. It had the sweetest smelling flowers on the sides of its hills. Although the villagers worked hard, they were poor. They were so poor that no one dared to name the village. They feared that if they chose the wrong name it would bring them bad luck. To them, it was just home. It was the only village in China left unnamed, but Chiang-An still loved it dearly.

The other dragons laughed at Chiang-An because of his affection for this village, but he did not care. Chiang-An loved to take out the bright, shiny pearl hidden under his chin and play with it in the sky at night. To the villagers below, his pearl looked like a falling star, or a passing comet.

Chiang-An loved to hear the villagers play their fiddles. They would play the most beautiful songs at night as Chiang-An watched them from the sky above. Like other Chinese dragons, he had the head of a camel, horns of a deer, eyes of a rabbit, ears of a bull, neck like a snake, belly of a frog, paws of a tiger, claws of an eagle, and scales like a carp.

One day the four Imperial dragons of China came to visit the unnamed village. Their visit was a rare honor and all the dragons gathered around. The elder dragons welcomed the Imperial dragons while Chiang-An watched with fascination.

"We come in preparation for the Year of the Dragon," said Tian Long, the Celestial Dragon. Like the other Imperial dragons, Tian Long had five toes while common dragons had only three or four. "It is especially important because it falls on the Chinese year 4698. However, many people around the world know it as the year 2000, a very auspicious number and the start of a new millennium."

"Every thousand years we pick one dragon to become a keeper of a mountain," said Shen Long, the Spirit Dragon. "Being a keeper of a mountain is important because the villagers will honor that dragon. We have chosen this village because it is the only one left unnamed in China." All the dragons wished to be chosen and become the keeper of the unnamed village's mountain. It was the first time any other dragons had shown any interest in the poor village.

"You are to bring gifts to the villagers to show your worthiness to become the keeper of their mountain," said Di Long, the dragon of land, stream, and river.

"The gifts must be able to last a thousand years," said Futsang Long, the Treasure Dragon. "Whoever brings the best gifts for this unnamed village will forever bring it prosperity and be given the honor of naming the village."

"Go now," said the Imperial dragons. "Come back on New Year's Eve of the Year of the Dragon."

The four Imperial dragons then blew out a thick mist from their mouths and disappeared. The other dragons also flew away to search for treasures all over China. Some found jade, while others found diamonds and gold. Since they were bigger and more experienced than he was, Chiang-An knew he had little chance of finding any treasures in China.

Little Chiang-An did not know what to do. How could he ever hope to find gifts to make him worthy of becoming a keeper of a mountain? Suddenly, he had an idea. He would search outside of China. This terrified him at first, for he had never left the little village, let alone China. But, he knew this was something he had to do. Reluctantly, Chiang-An tucked his pearl back under his chin and left China far behind. He flew for many days in search of the perfect gift for the villagers.

Chiang-An finally began to tire and took a rest in England. He found a large clock tower named Big Ben that overlooked the Thames River. It was night and the clock was lit up.

Just as Chiang-An was thinking how peaceful and quiet it was, the giant bell inside Big Ben began to ring. It surprised Chiang-An and he flew off hastily. Soon he found himself in the countryside, where he came upon a strange ring of stones called Stonehenge. There he was met by a huge, winged dragon.

"Who may you be?" bellowed the fierce dragon in a deep, surly voice. The dragon had a long tail and forked tongue. Most fearsome was the fire that breathed from his mouth and nostrils. Chiang-An, seeing the fire, was impressed, and thought that this dragon must have treasures beyond imagination.

"Oh, Dragon of England, I see how powerful you are," said Chiang-An. "You must surely have a gift for me to give the villagers in China where I live. It will be a gift to them for the New Year."

"So, you think because I am powerful that I have treasures?" asked the dragon.

Chiang-An nodded.

"Then I had better tell you a story," said the dragon. "There was once a very greedy dragon who lived in the town of Silene. This dragon breathed poison and killed all the animals and crops."

"What did the villagers do? " asked Chiang-An.

"The King, in desperation, agreed to sacrifice a child every day in hopes of pleasing this dreadful dragon," continued the dragon. "Then one day, it was his own daughter's turn to be killed. Luckily, a tall knight, named George, came riding by."

"Did George kill the greedy dragon?" asked Chiang-An.

"Yes," answered the dragon. "Later, he was adopted by medieval crusaders as their patron saint and became known as St. George,

protector of England, Catalonia, Italy, Greece, and Aragon. Even though he was a dragon slayer, I have come to admire St. George because he fought for goodness and justice. I have also learned how to be humble. So whenever you look up into the stars, you can hear my song of honor for people like St. George." The dragon then sang a beautiful song as he flew up to the stars.

On the ground the Dragon of England had left a sword. When Chiang-An swung the sword, the sound reminded him of Big Ben. Chiang-An listened to the song and became more confused. What did the sword mean? Did the dragon tell this story because he wanted to keep his real treasures hidden? Chiang-An was hoping for unusual gold or jade, not a song and a sword. Nevertheless, he tucked the sword under his chin along with the pearl.

Chiang-An flew off to his next destination. After several days he glided down next to a long river called Likouala in the Congo area of Africa. It was very hot because Likouala was located on the equator. Chiang-An was taking a drink of water to cool himself off when he felt the earth shake. Out from the lake came a huge dragon, frightening Chiang-An. The dragon had the body of an elephant, and its small head rested on a long, slender neck. Her four massive legs rocked the earth when she walked.

"Another visitor to Likouala," laughed the dragon. "You are not even human. What may you be?"

"My name is Chiang-An. I am a dragon from China. I come in search of a gift for my villagers to celebrate the New Year."

"Ho, ho," shouted the dragon. "I am called Mokele-mbembe. I am the keeper of Likouala."

Chiang-An thought that Mokele-mbembe must be a very powerful dragon to be a keeper of such a long river. "Tell me, oh Mokele-mbembe," implored Chiang-An, "what great gift do you have to merit being a keeper of Likouala?"

"I have the greatest gift of all," explained Mokele-mbembe. "Visitors come from all over the world to find me. They want to capture me, but I am too elusive. In their quests to find me, they have made discoveries that helped create the great Kongo civilization of Central Africa. Some people have spent their whole lives looking for me, but I will never let them find me."

"Why not?" asked Chiang-An. "You could give someone the gift of glory and fame."

"Ha, ha! You are wrong," laughed Mokele-mbembe. "It is the quest that is the gift."

"Do they not get so frustrated that they leave?" asked Chiang-An.

"Ho, ho. Some do," laughed Mokele-mbembe. "But not before they hear my song. My song reminds them to always follow their hearts. Once they hear it, they will always remember the fun they had searching for me."

Mokele-mbembe then sang a song into the wind.

Suddenly she stopped. "I must go now. Humans are coming. Good luck, Dragon of China. I leave you with this small gift for the villagers."

It was a scroll with writing on it. Mokele-mbembe sank back into the river. Chiang-An did not want to be seen, either, so he tucked the scroll under his chin with the sword and the pearl and flew off.

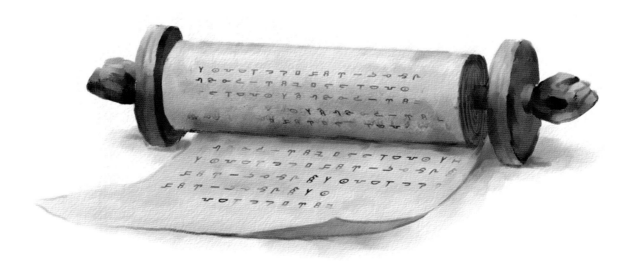

Chiang-An crossed a large ocean and landed on the shore of the great Lake Ontario in North America. He enjoyed listening to the gentle rolling sound of the waves. In the distance he could hear the sound of the thundering cascades of Niagara Falls. These falls were so great that they bordered on two countries, Canada and the United States. He noticed that the sound became louder and louder until, suddenly, a large serpent dragon swam up to him.

"Who are you?" asked a frightened Chiang-An.

"I am the great Serpent Dragon," roared the dragon with the loudness of Niagara Falls. "I am known in the myths among the Iroquois of the Five Nations."

"Of course you are part of their myths, because you are so large that you could surely kill all of them in one giant swallow," said Chiang-An. He quaked in awe as he observed that the serpent dragon was easily three times as large as he was. "They must certainly shower you with gifts. Perhaps you might spare one so that I could return to China? I will give it to the villagers as a gift for the New Year."

Suddenly, Serpent Dragon's eyes saddened. She looked down and spoke softly. Chiang-An noticed the change and relaxed.

"You are right," said Serpent Dragon. "I did kill many before, but nevermore."

"What made you change?" asked Chiang-An.

"I wasn't always so large," said Serpent Dragon. "In fact, I was once quite small and was raised by a little Iroquois girl. As I grew larger, I began to use my size to tease and frighten people. One day I made loud noises and threatened to eat the villagers, so they locked themselves behind the gates of their stockade. I opened my mouth so wide that they thought they were walking into a cave. The little girl

begged me to stop, but I did not. She then took out a bow and arrow and shot me with a magic medicine. As I fell toward the lake, the people came out of my mouth and ran for safety. While the villagers were celebrating, the little girl was crying."

"Why?" asked a puzzled Chiang-An.

"Because she still loved me," said Serpent Dragon. "I was so ashamed. Whenever the Iroquois hear the loud roar of Niagara Falls, it is really my song. I remind them that no matter how powerful you become, you must remember to treat others with kindness."

The great Serpent Dragon sang a bit of her powerful song before descending back into Lake Ontario. Chiang-An noticed that just before she disappeared beneath the water's bright surface, she flung an old coin to the shore. Chiang-An flew off, puzzled by the words of the large Iroquois Serpent Dragon. He was equally confused by her gift. So far he had a sword, a scroll, and an old coin.

Chiang-An next flew to Teotihuacan, just outside of Mexico City. He saw the great pyramids of the Moon and Sun, which were made before the arrival of the Europeans in that part of the world. Most fascinating to Chiang-An were the carvings of a plumed serpent on the Pyramid of Quetzalcoatl. The nobility of the beast stunned Chiang-An. After a rest, he flew to the eastern shores of Mexico. He looked up to the stars and wondered how long it would take before he could find a gift worthy to show the Imperial dragons.

Chiang-An fell asleep, but was suddenly awakened by a large, bright green dragon riding toward him on a raft of entwined serpents. The dragon's belly was scarlet, and his body was covered with beautiful feathers. Chiang-An recognized the dragon as the same one he had seen pictured in the carvings at Teotihuacan. Surely this dragon is of royal blood and will have a gift for me, he said to himself.

I am Quetzalcoatl, plumed serpent god of wind, wisdom, and life," declared the dragon. "I am able to hear your dreams, so I know all about your journey."

"You can read my dreams?" asked an amazed Chiang-An. "Then you must know that I am seeking a gift for the villagers where I live. If the four Imperial dragons think it worthy, I will be honored by the villagers for a thousand years."

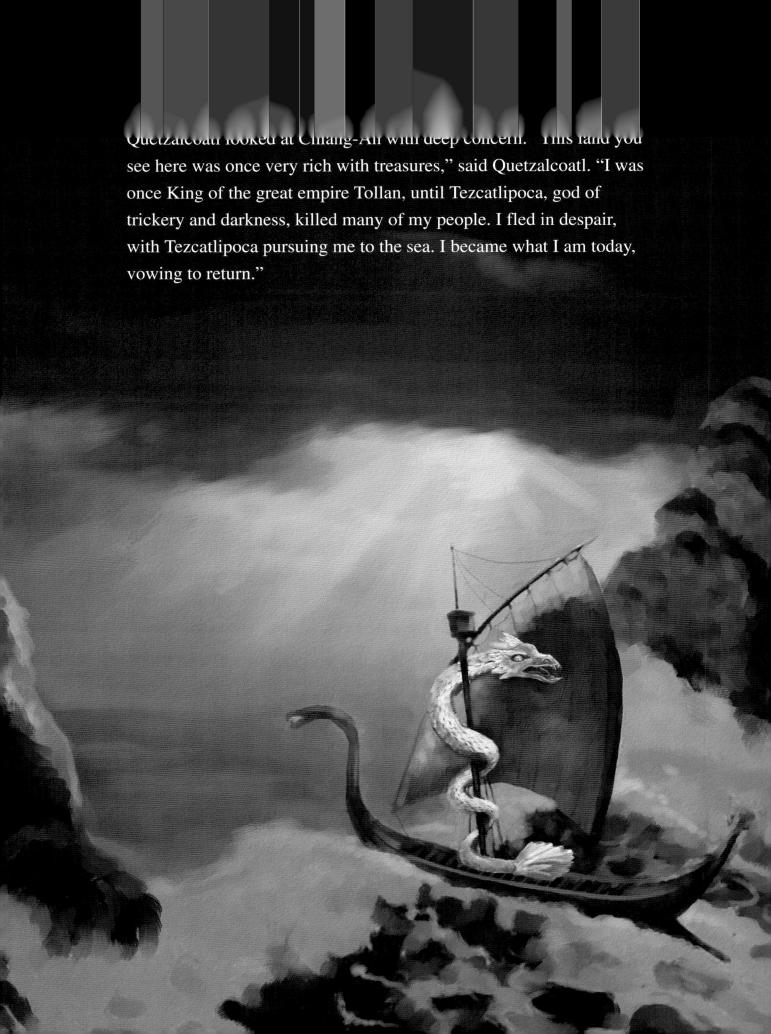

Quetzalcoatl looked at Chiang-Ali with deep concern. "This land you see here was once very rich with treasures," said Quetzalcoatl. "I was once King of the great empire Tollan, until Tezcatlipoca, god of trickery and darkness, killed many of my people. I fled in despair, with Tezcatlipoca pursuing me to the sea. I became what I am today, vowing to return."

"Now my people are scattered throughout the Americas," continued Quetzalcoatl. "I sing to them in their dreams to keep the faith. They must believe they can overcome any struggle they face. They must hold onto the hope that we will someday return to greatness. Many people hear my song and think it is just a dream. But a dream of hope is a very powerful treasure. Take that message to your villagers in China."

Quetzalcoatl sang a song of inspiration for Chiang-An. He then slithered toward his raft of serpents and climbed aboard. As the raft flowed out to sea, Chiang-An saw that the feathered beast had left something behind for him. It was a cup made from the same stone that was found on the Pyramid of Quetzalcoatl.

The next thing Chiang-An knew he was awakening to the sound of the surf. Was it just a dream, or was it real? Chiang-An thought of the English dragon, of Mokele-mbembe, of the great Serpent Dragon, and now, of Quetzalcoatl. He looked at the sword, the scroll, the old coin, and the stone cup, and remembered each of the dragons' songs. Chiang-An then realized what he must do and how he would present his gifts.

He flew up to the sky and back to China. By the time Chiang-An returned, all the other dragons had finished offering their gifts for the Imperial dragons to see. Chiang-An had never seen so many precious gifts. Surely the other dragons had brought enough riches to make any village prosperous for the next thousand years. All Chiang-An had were his four strange gifts from foreign lands.

"Chiang-An, what gifts do you bring for the villagers?" asked Futsang Long.

Chiang-An nervously stepped forward. He desperately hoped that his gifts would be good enough. Looking up at the four giant Imperial dragons, he brought out the stone cup, the sword, the scroll, and the old coin for all to see. The other dragons began to snicker.

"What kind of gifts are these?" laughed one dragon.

"These gifts represent places where my image will be carved all over the village." Chiang-An replied. "Dragons will be carved in nine places. These nine places will remind the villagers that I, Chiang-An, am here."

Chiang-An first showed the Imperial dragons the stone cup. "This stone cup represents the pillars that hold up the buildings in the village," he said solemnly. "A first dragon image will be carved on those pillars. The cup shape represents the life that water brings; therefore, a second dragon will be carved on the beams of bridges."

He then took out the sword from the English dragon. "A third dragon image will be carved on the handles of swords to help the villagers defend themselves from enemies. A fourth dragon will be carved on bells and gongs," he said. He then swung the sword and made the sound of Big Ben. "The sound represents the bells and gongs that will ring loudly to warn the villagers of attack."

Chiang-An took out the scroll from under his chin. "The words written on this scroll tell many wonderful stories. A fifth dragon will be carved on stone tablets to represent literature. The words will be found in the temples for the villagers to learn. A sixth dragon will be carved on the rooftops of those temples."

Lastly, he took out the old coin and flipped it into the air. "This coin represents the many decisions in life that we all have to make. A seventh dragon will be carved on prison gates to represent the dangers of making poor choices, and another will be carved on the thrones of Buddha to represent the wise choices."

"This is all very interesting," chuckled one of the larger dragons as he interrupted Chiang-An. "But how will the villagers prosper for the next thousand years from these simple carvings of dragons around the village? How can they compare to the gold, jewels, and jade that I brought?"

Chiang-An drew himself up to respond. "Honorable Imperial dragons, I bring the gift that this village will need most to prosper for the next thousand years. I bring hope. The carvings represent the hopes and dreams that these villagers need. They will be given this hope whenever they hear my last gift, a song."

Chiang-An then sang the most beautiful song any dragon had ever heard. He had taken the themes and melodies of each of the four dragon songs and woven them into one. It was a song of honor and justice. It was a song of power, inspiration, and great beauty. It was a song that could make a person humble but also fill a person's mind with curiosity, making him anxious to explore and invent. It was a song that reminded people in times of struggle to keep their faith; and that no matter how far they traveled, they would always have a home to return to.

"How will the villagers hear this song?" asked an intrigued Shen Long.

"I will sing it to them whenever they look up into the stars," replied Chiang-An. "My song will be carried in the wind as it comes down the valley. The villagers will hear it in the great roar of waterfalls, and in their dreams at night. It will give them hope for a brighter tomorrow."

The four Imperial dragons were very pleased with the gifts, especially the song. They all agreed that Chiang-An deserved to be Keeper of the Mountain.

"Since you are now Keeper of the Mountain, you have the honor of naming the village," said Shen Long.

Chiang-An had a name all picked out. "I would like to name the village Fragrant Mountain, for the village will be known by the sweet smells of the flowers on its mountain."

"Good name," the four Imperial dragons agreed.

"Wait," said Tian Long. "You said that the image of the dragon will be carved in nine places. I only counted eight. Where is the ninth?"

Chiang-An whispered the answer back. After hearing him, the four Imperial dragons all smiled.

From that day on, throughout the new millennium, Fragrant Mountain prospered. Chiang-An could hear his song sung in operas, sung in schools, and sung even while people worked in the fields. He liked it most when he could peer down from the sky and hear his favorite fiddle music. The villagers honored Chiang-An by carving the ninth dragon image around the screws of all their fiddles. And as the fiddles were played, dragonsong would fill every corner of Fragrant Mountain in the southeast corner of China.

# Dragonsong

Carry my song, oh gentle winds
Through the vast, verdant valleys, and over the hills.
It is a song of quest and adventure
For everyone to hear.

The bards speak softly in the night
As they gaze upon the stars so high above,
Of a song of honor and justice
In those desperate, lonely times.

Yet the power of the greatest waterfall
Cannot convey its message loud enough,
To remain forever humbled and grateful
To those who carried your burdens past.

So dream my song lest you forget
That your greatest days still lie ahead.
For a thousand years this song of hope
Is for everyone to hear.

*To Liling, my wife, and my two best dragon sons, Christopher and Brandon*
-R.Y.-

*To Jane, my wife*
-C.C.-

*To our faithful readers around the world*
-Publisher-

**Shen's Books**
40951 Fremont Blvd. Fremont, CA 94538
800-456-6660
http://www.shens.com

Library of Congress Cataloging-in-Publication Data
Young, Russell.
Dragonsong : a fable for the new millennium / written by Russell Young ; illustrated by Civi Cheng.
p. cm.
Summary: As Chiang-An, a small Chinese dragon, travels the world in search of a special enduring
gift for his village, he meets four other dragons,
each of whom gives him a song, an unusual gift, and words of wisdom.
ISBN 1-885008-12-0
[1. Dragons--Fiction. 2. Gifts--Fiction. 3. Conduct of life--Fiction. 4. China--Fiction.]
I. Cheng, Civi, ill. II. Title.
PZ7.Y8769Dr2000   [Fic]--dc21   99-045351
10 9 8 7 6 5 4 3 2